The Troll from the Mill

Maureen Haselhurst
Illustrated by Garry Parsons

RIGBY

The troll from the mill . . .

ran up the hill.

He got to the top . . .

4

and saw Big Boss the Bull!

"Buzz off!" said Big Boss.

7

The troll from the mill
rolled back down the hill!